My Sister, Alicia May

Written by Nancy Tupper Ling

Illustrated by Shennen Bersani

"*My Sister, Alicia May* is a delightful book perfect for siblings and peers of children with Down syndrome and other disabilities. Beautifully illustrated, this book is a must for every school library!"

–David Tolleson, Executive Director National Down Syndrome Congress

Pleasant St. Press

For Alicia and Rachel—my inspiration,
and for Vincent, Elizabeth and Sarah—my motivation. *Soli Deo Gloria.*
—NTL

I grew up with one younger sister. Her name is Holly and she has Down syndrome. When my editor asked me to illustrate this book, she had no idea of my background. In shock I listened as she described the book, and in disbelief she listened when I told her that my own personal story matched that of the protagonist, Rachel. On a warm spring day, I met and fell in love with Alicia May. But it was in young Rachel, whose joys and frustrations were like my own when I was her age, that I found a kindred spirit. With love and admiration I dedicate this book to Rachel Crossley.
—SB

More Titles from Pleasant St. Press

Off I Go!
New Old Shoes
That Kind of Dog
Little Shrew Caboose
Your Tummy's Talking!
The Warmest Place of All
On a Dark, Dark Night
My Sister, Alicia May
The Zoopendous Surprise
Farmer Brown and His Little Red Truck
If a Monkey Jumps Onto Your School Bus

Text copyright Nancy Tupper Ling © 2009
Illustrations copyright Shennen Bersani © 2009

ISBN: 978-0-9792035-9-6
Library of Congress Control Number: 2008924640

10 9 8 7 6 5 4 3 2 1

Printed and bound in the USA

Published by Pleasant St. Press
PO Box 520
Raynham Center, MA 02768 USA

www.pleasantstpress.com
E-mail: info@pleasantstpress.com

Book Design by Jill Ronsley, www.suneditwrite.com

BANG! Every morning Alicia May throws open my bedroom door. *Crack!* The "Stay Out!" sign falls to the floor.

"Here I am!" she cries. "Shine and rise!"

Alicia May is special. I know. I'm her big sister.
Some people say her special needs make
her special, but I know she's special
for many reasons.

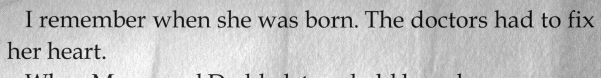

I remember when she was born. The doctors had to fix her heart.

When Mama and Daddy let me hold her, she was warm and heavy in my arms. She looked like a tiny astronaut with tubes sticking out of her body and wires attached to her baby-soft skin. But she didn't cry. She was very brave.

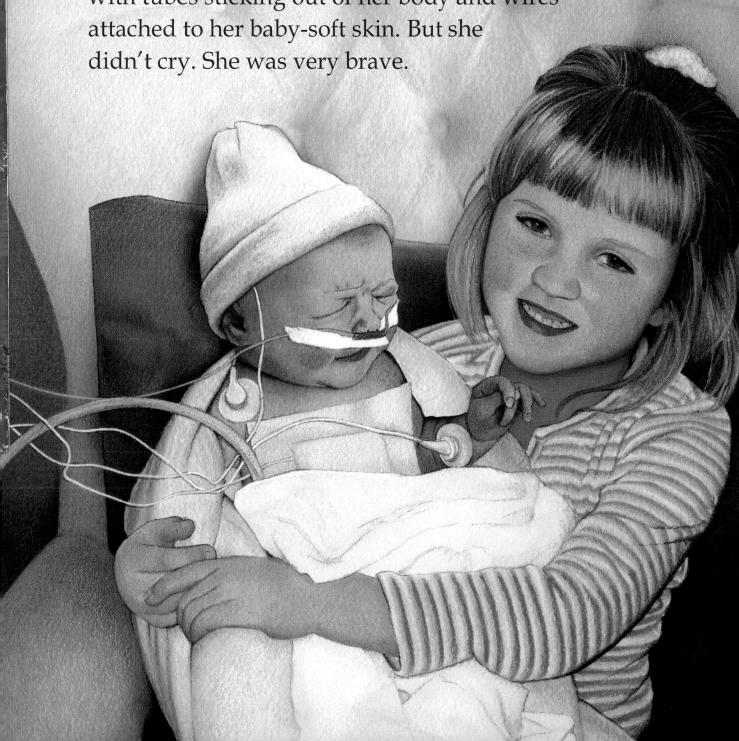

In some ways, my sister is like any six-year-old girl.
She likes dogs and horses.

She likes to paint her
toenails with polka dots,
and she loves bugs.

She peers long and hard at crickets and June bugs and dragonflies. She watches ladybugs warm themselves on our red door.

Then she counts their dots: "One lady dot, two lady dot, three lady dot …"

I think God is glad someone notices these things.

Alicia May doesn't like to leave a place she really loves. My friend Katie has a train set in her basement. Once, Alicia May watched the train for what seemed like forever. She followed it as it passed through the mountain and over the bridge again and again. When it was time to go home, she screamed, "NOT GOING! I'M NOT GOING!"

She cried until my head hurt.

That's when Katie and I grabbed the caboose and put it in her hands.

"Keep this," Katie said.

"'Til next time," I added.

Alicia smiled. "Okay, Rae-Rae," she said. "Thanks."

Alicia May is funny. She talks to the animals at the zoo. "Hi-ya, Foxy Mama," she says to a fox. "Hi-ya, Stinky Butt," she says to a skunk.

When we leave, she stands under the "Welcome to the Zoo" sign and waves goodbye.

"Nice seeing you," we say together. I taught her that.

My sister has a sharp memory.
She remembers how many steps lead to the library.

She remembers to wake us up
every morning. And she always
remembers people she meets.

Every day she and Mama
go for the mail.

They walk to the end of the street where Mrs. Scotti lives. Mrs. Scotti waits for them and waves from her window. On warm summer days, I hear Alicia May shouting on Mrs. Scotti's front porch, "Hi-ya, Mrs. Scotti." Mrs. Scotti likes that.

I don't always play with my sister. I have my own friends. After school, Katie rides her bike to our house. We head down the dirt road to the covered bridge and drop pebbles into the river—KERPLUNK!—until we hear Alicia May.

"Rae-Rae!" she calls. "It's home time."

We pedal home and find Alicia May waiting for us.
She hugs us both as though we've been gone forever.

Some days, I don't think my sister's special at all.
Some days, she annoys me so much that I don't want
her around me.

Some days, I'm sick of watching out for her, like the first time she rode the school bus with me. The boys in the back of the bus were mean to her. They shouted, "Stand!" and Alicia May stood up. They shouted, "Scream peanut butter!" and she screamed, "Peanut butter!" I slouched down in my seat beside Katie.

"Katie," I whispered, "pretend we don't know her."
So we did.

The boys were mean for three days until I stood up and yelled, "You yellow-bellied pipsqueaks! Knock it off!"
And they did.
Alicia May gave me a big hug across the aisle. "You rock," she said.

Alicia May doesn't like her breathing machine. Some nights, when Mama and Daddy ask me to help, I play "Steamy the Dragon" with her

"Come on, cutie," I coax. "Steamy the Dragon wants to kiss you goodnight."

I make Steamy tickle her nose.

"NO!" she warns.

"For me?" I ask.

"All right, Rae-Rae," she says. "One steamy puff."

"Just one!" I smile.

After Alicia May falls asleep, Mama
comes to my room. She pulls my fluffy
quilt over me, tucks me in and gives me
a hug to let me know she loves me.

"What's my big girl thinking?"
she asks.

I snuggle way down under my covers. I keep thinking.

"Hmmm?" Mama tries again.

"Well," I reply "I wish everyone had an Alicia May. But
then Alicia May wouldn't be special, would she?"

Mama bends down and kisses me. She turns off the lamp.
"Special like you, Rachel," she says, as she moves towards
the door. "Special like you!"